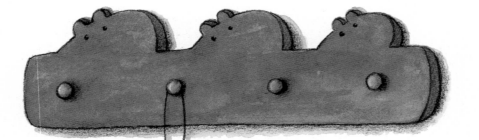

a minedition *book*
published *by* Penguin Young Readers Group

Text copyright © 2004 *by* Brigitte Weninger
Illustrations copyright © 2004 *by* Stephanie Roehe
First American edition, 2005
First published in German under the original title:
MIKO „Waschen? NEIN!"
translated *by* Charise Myngheer
Coproduction with Michael Neugebauer
Publishing Ltd. Hong Kong.

Published simultaneously in Canada.
ISBN 0-698-40013-5

Manufactured in Hong Kong *by* Wide World Ltd.
Designed *by* Michael Neugebauer
Typesetting in Kidprint MT
Color separation *by* Fotoreproduzioni Grafiche, Verona, Italy.
Library of Congress Cataloging-in-Publication Data available *upon* request.

10 9 8 7 6 5 4 3 2 1
First Impression

Brigitte Weninger

MiKO

"No Bath! No Way!"

Illustrated by
Stephanie Roehe

minedition

Miko and his little friend Mimiki had played outside all day.
"Oh my, you two look like you had fun today!" said Mom. "You
need a bath."
Miko made a face and grumbled.

When the tub was full, Mom called
for Miko, but he didn't answer.

"Strange," said Mom when
she saw little Mimiki sitting
on the floor alone.
"I wonder where Miko went?

"Hmmm," thought Mom. "I bet Miko will *be* hungry when he gets back. I think I'll surprise him with his favorite meal."

Soon the whole house smelled like sweet
cinnamon toast.
But Miko still hadn't come back.

"That's too bad," Mom said to Mimiki. "We'll have to eat it all ourselves."

"RRRRRRRH!" Suddenly, a deep growling and scratching sound came from the closet.

"Do you hear that?" asked Mom.

"RRRRRRRH...SCRAAATCH...RRRRRRRH..."

"Do you think it's a monster?" whispered Mom. "It sounds dangerous! Maybe it's just hungry!"

Mom put a piece of toast on a plate and set it in front of the door.
Suddenly, a dirty-gray paw reached out and grabbed it. She put another
piece on the plate and it disappeared as quickly as the first.
"It must be starving!" said Mom. "Maybe it will join us for dinner."
Carefully Mom opened the door.

"Miko! There you are!" Mom said, surprised. "What are you doing in the closet?" "I'm hiding," said Miko. I don't want to take a bath! NO BATH! NO WAY!"

"But you always take a bath," said Mom.

"But today is special!" Miko said.

Look, I have silver sand on my arms."

He stretched his paws out under the light so she could see the glistening grains of sand.

"And I caught two balls! I've never been that good before!"

"What's all over your face?" asked Mom.

"It's ice cream. Mina bought it for me," Miko said, smiling.

"It had sprinkles. It was the best ice cream ever!"

"Today was perfect!" said Miko. "I don't want it to be over!"

"Okay," said Mom. "But you're too dirty to sleep in your clean bed.

Would you two like to sleep on the floor tonight?"

"Yes!" answered Miko excitedly. "It will be like camping!"

Mom fed Miko his cinnamon toast so he wouldn't mess up his silver-sanded paws. Then she made a bed on the floor. "Good night!" said Mom. "Good night," called Miko as he cuddled with Mimiki.

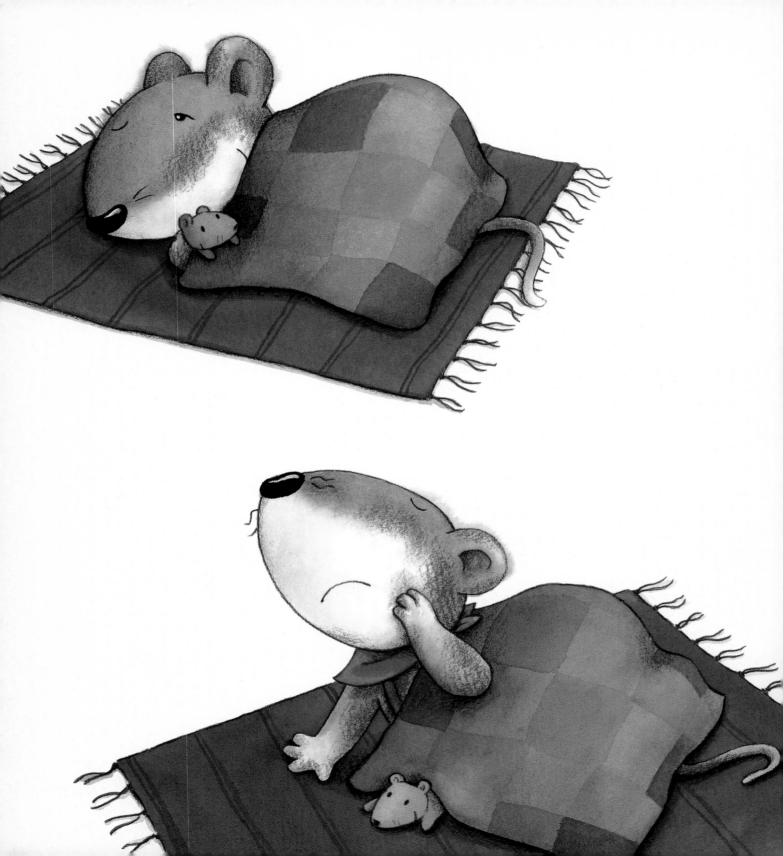

Miko closed his eyes, but he couldn't fall asleep.
His clothes began to scratch and tickle.
The ice cream on his chin began to itch.
And the floor felt really hard.
"But I don't want to take a bath!" thought Miko.
"NO BATH! NO WAY! If I take a bath, then my perfect day
will be over." He thought a minute.
"I have a great idea!" shouted Miko. "Come on, Mimiki."

Mom heard water splashing.

Curiously, she looked into the bathroom.

Miko and Mimiki were sitting in the bathtub, all soaped up.

"So?" asked Mom. "You changed your mind?"

"Yes, I did!" glowed Miko. "I had a great idea! If I take a bath today, I can just do all this great stuff again tomorrow! It'll be perfect!"

For more information about MIKO and our other books and the authors and artists who created them, please visit our website: **www.minedition.com**